**SPORTS INJURIES:
HOW TO PREVENT, DIAGNOSE, & TREAT**

CHEERLEADING

Sports Injuries:
How to Prevent, Diagnose, & Treat

- Baseball
- Basketball
- Cheerleading
- Equestrian
- Extreme Sports
- Field
- Field Hockey
- Football
- Gymnastics
- Hockey
- Ice Skating
- Lacrosse
- Soccer
- Track
- Volleyball
- Weight Training
- Wrestling

SPORTS INJURIES:
HOW TO PREVENT, DIAGNOSE, & TREAT

CHEERLEADING

LISA McCOY

MASON CREST PUBLISHERS
www.masoncrest.com

Mason Crest Publishers Inc.
370 Reed Road
Broomall, PA 19008
(866) MCP-BOOK (toll free)
www.masoncrest.com

Copyright © 2004 Mason Crest Publishers, Inc.

All rights reserved. No part of this publication may be reproduced or transmitted in any form or by any means, electronic or mechanical, including photocopying, recording, taping, or any information storage and retrieval system, without permission in writing from the publisher.

First printing

1 2 3 4 5 6 7 8 9 10

Library of Congress Cataloging-in-Publication Data on file
at the Library of Congress

ISBN 1-59084-628-1

Series ISBN 1-59084-625-7

Editorial and design by
Amber Books Ltd.
Bradley's Close
74–77 White Lion Street
London N1 9PF
www.amberbooks.co.uk

Project Editor: Michael Spilling
Design: Graham Curd
Picture Research: Natasha Jones

Printed and bound in the Hashemite Kingdom of Jordan

PICTURE CREDITS
Corbis: 6, 8, 10, 11, 12, 13, 14, 16, 19, 20, 23, 24, 32–33, 34, 36, 38, 39, 40, 42, 47, 50, 52, 54, 55, 56, 58.

FRONT COVER: Corbis (br, bl); Topham Picturepoint (tr, tl).

ILLUSTRATIONS: Courtesy of Amber Books except:
Bright Star Publishing plc: 43, 45, 48;
Tony Randell: 26, 28, 29, 30.

IMPORTANT NOTICE

This book is intended to provide general information about sports injuries, their prevention, and their treatment. The information contained herein is not intended as a substitute for professional medical care. Always consult a doctor before beginning any exercise program, and for diagnosis and treatment of any injury. Accordingly, the publisher cannot accept any responsibility for any prosecution or proceedings brought or instituted against any person or body as a result of the use or misuse of the techniques and information within.

CONTENTS

Foreword	6
The History of Cheerleading	8
Mental Preparation to Avoid Injury	16
Warm-Up Exercises to Avoid Injury	24
Equipment	34
Common Injuries and Treatment	40
Careers in Cheerleading	52
Glossary	60
Further Information	62
Index	64

Foreword

Sports Injuries: How to Prevent, Diagnose, and Treat is a seventeen-volume series written for young people who are interested in learning about various sports and how to participate in them safely. Each volume examines the history of the sport and the rules of play; it also acts as a guide for prevention and treatment of injuries, and includes instruction on stretching, warming up, and strength training, all of which can help players avoid the most common musculoskeletal injuries. *Sports Injuries* offers ways for readers to improve their performance and gain more enjoyment from playing sports, and young athletes will find these volumes informative and helpful in their pursuit of excellence.

Sports medicine professionals assigned to a sport that they are not familiar with can also benefit from this series. For example, a football athletic trainer may need to provide medical care for a local gymnastics meet. Although the emergency medical principles and action plan would remain the same, the athletic trainer could provide better care for the gymnasts after reading a simple overview of the principles of gymnastics in *Sports Injuries*.

Although these books offer an overview, they are not intended to be comprehensive in the recognition and management of sports injuries. The text helps the reader appreciate and gain awareness of the common injuries possible during participation in sports. Reference material and directed readings are provided for those who want to delve further into the subject.

Written in a direct and easily accessible style, *Sports Injuries* is an enjoyable series that will help young people learn about sports and sports medicine.

Susan Saliba, Ph.D., National Athletic Trainers' Association Education Council

Even though cheerleading has been around since the 1870s, it is more popular today than ever.

The History of Cheerleading

Cheerleading—the pom-poms, the outfits, the yells—is a sport so closely linked with high school and college as to be almost inseparable. Many a teenage girl has dreamed of being a cheerleader. Not that this sport is just for women—many college teams are mixed, and, what's more, the first cheerleaders were men.

Sometime in the 1870s, Thomas Peebler gathered six men on the sidelines of a Princeton University football game and led them in an organized yell before the student body. According to records, the yell went as follows: "Ray, Ray, Ray! Tiger, Tiger, Tiger! Sis, Sis, Sis! Boom, Boom, Boom! Aaaaaaah! Princeton, Princeton, Princeton!"

In 1884, Peebler shared this yell with the University of Minnesota. The student body here quickly adopted it, and, on November 2, 1898, a young man by the name of Johnny Campbell got so excited by the yell that he left his seat and went to stand in front of the crowd, jumping and waving his arms in excitement.

Later, the university introduced the first organized cheerleaders and the first official "fight song." The first cheerleading **fraternity**, known as Gamma Sigma, was formed there in 1900.

Perharps surprisingly for some, the first "cheerleader" was actually a man by the name of Johnny Campbell at the University of Minnesota in 1884.

CHEERLEADING

Early cheerleading equipment included such things as drums and whistles. The megaphone became a standard piece of cheerleading equipment in the early 1900s.

Cheerleading equipment became standardized during the early twentieth century. At first, team spirits had been roused by drums and noisemakers, such as the horns and whistles used for New Year's Eve parties. These were now replaced by the **megaphone** and the pom-pom. Megaphones, which had been used sporadically in cheerleading since the sport's beginning, became a popular staple of cheerleading squads. Pom-poms were introduced in the 1930s, made originally from paper. The pom-poms of today, made from vinyl, were introduced in 1965 by Fred Gastoff and later adopted by the International Cheerleading Foundation (now known as the World Cheerleading Association).

THE HISTORY OF CHEERLEADING

In the 1920s, women began to take an active interest in cheerleading. At the same time, the components of cheerleading began to change. No longer content with just leading yells, cheerleaders of the '30s and '40s incorporated gymnastics and tumbling into their cheer routines. Cheerleading continued to evolve throughout the '40s and '50s. For example, regulations and standards for cheers and stunts were put into place, and more and more women were taking part. In 1948, Laurence "Hurkie" Hurkimer organized the first cheerleading camp at Sam Houston University in Huntsville, Texas. Fifty-two girls attended, and the camp was considered quite a success. Hurkimer went on to found the National Cheerleading Association, and he also created several slogans, ribbons, and buttons that cheerleading teams sold to raise both student spirit and much-needed funds.

Cheerleading became increasingly important at schools and colleges throughout the United States. By the 1950s, other colleges were conducting cheerleading workshops to teach basic cheerleading skills. In 1967, the first ranking of the Top Ten College Cheer Squads was released, and the first Cheerleaders All America award ceremony was held by the International Cheerleading Foundation (ICF). That same year, the Baltimore Colts football team organized the first professional cheerleading squad.

In 1972, professional cheerleading was raised to

Women began to participate in cheerleading in the 1920s. Increasing interest led to the first cheerleading camp in Texas in 1948.

11

CHEERLEADING

As the twentieth century progressed, cheerleading teams became more structured, with standard rules and regulations, official uniforms, and choreographed dance moves becoming part of cheerleading.

a new level by a Texan, Tex Schramm. Traditionally, women stood on the sidelines yelling cheers. Now Schramm had the idea of forming the cheerleaders into a squad of dancers, who would serve to complement and support the actual football game. Auditions were held and training began. The "new and improved" Dallas Cowboys cheerleaders were introduced in the 1972–1973 N.F.L. season, and a new form of entertainment was born.

Prior to the 1970s, cheerleaders had primarily supported a school's football and basketball teams. During the 1970s, however, cheerleaders began to support a

THE HISTORY OF CHEERLEADING

FAMOUS CHEERLEADERS

Many famous people, including politicians, actors, and singers, have also been cheerleaders. Some of the names might surprise you:

- Paula Abdul
- Madonna
- Halle Berry
- Steve Martin
- Sandra Bullock
- Reba McIntyre
- George W. Bush
- Luke Perry
- Jamie Lee Curtis
- Ronald Reagan
- Kirk Douglas
- Franklin D. Roosevelt
- Dwight D. Eisenhower
- Cybill Shepherd
- Sally Field
- Jimmy Stewart
- Teri Hatcher
- Meryl Streep
- Samuel L. Jackson
- Racquel Welch

More than just an award-winning actress, film star Halle Berry was also an accomplished cheerleader.

13

wide variety of other sports, including wrestling, track, swimming, and volleyball. At some schools, the same cheer squad supported all these teams; larger schools formed separate squads for each sport.

In 1978, with the support of the ICF, CBS-TV broadcast the first nationally televised Collegiate Cheerleading Championships. In 1976, the Dallas Cowboys Cheerleaders performed at Super Bowl X, thereby starting a trend, both among other professional teams and among high school and university squads, for an emphasis on dance routines in cheerleading.

Today, cheerleading is a recognized sport around the world. Japan, Australia, Canada, and Mexico, not to mention an increasing number of European countries, have all gotten into the cheerleading spirit. There are competitions at

Before he became the leader of the United States, President George W. Bush was a leader of cheers. Here, he demonstrates the use of the megaphone.

FUN FACTS

- At the University of Kentucky, the average cheerleader is about 5 feet (1.5 m) and weighs 97 pounds (44 kg).
- About ninety-eight percent of all female cheerleaders are former gymnasts, compared to just twenty percent of male cheerleaders.
- Lila McCann, country music star, performed cheerleading routines for Elizabeth II, Queen of England.
- There are at least four million cheerleaders in thirty-one countries.
- Ninety-seven percent of all cheerleaders are female; however, almost fifty percent of collegiate cheerleaders are male.
- Twelve percent of cheerleaders are five to thirteen years old and twelve percent are dancers.
- Eighty-three percent of all cheerleaders have a B grade point average or better.
- Sixty-two percent of cheerleaders are involved in a second sport.
- Eighty percent of schools in the United States have cheerleading squads. The most popular sport for cheerleading is football.

Source: cheerleading.about.com

the middle school, high school, and college level, and universal standards and guidelines have been established. Training courses for cheerleading coaches and sponsors span the United States. Cheerleading has certainly come a long way since Johnny Campbell jumped out of his seat and rushed to the front of the student body in his excitement.

Mental Preparation to Avoid Injury

Preparation is a part of preventing any sports injury. This is no different for cheerleading, a sport that combines gymnastics, dance, and tumbling, and which takes place on a variety of surfaces, including asphalt, polished wood, and grass. Before picking up a set of pom-poms, you must first be properly stretched and warmed up.

The fact that the muscles of your body should be warmed up with stretches and other exercises before you begin is probably not new information. However, have you ever given thought to another important part of warming up: mental preparation? Mental preparation—exercises to improve concentration, awareness, and discipline—is just as important as physical preparation in the sport of cheerleading. This preparation can take many forms, including visualization, inspiration, goal-setting, attitude, developing a sense of humor, positive thinking, and **affirmations**.

VISUALIZATION

Visualization can be an effective means of mentally preparing yourself for a sport. For a long time, many people in the Western world believed that the mind and

Visualization—picturing yourself performing an activity in your mind's eye—can be of tremendous benefit to you as a cheerleader.

the body were two separate, distinct entities. However, we are now coming to understand more and more about the connection between the body and the mind. Indeed, they are not separate at all. Rather, what you think and how you feel correlates directly to the state of your body. In turn, how your body feels, or the messages it sends to your brain, affects your mental state. Take advantage of the link between the mind and the body when you are mentally preparing yourself for cheerleading.

Essentially, visualization means that you see yourself in your mind's eye performing an activity correctly and without injury. Suppose, for example, you are concerned about a new cheerleading routine that you have to master. Close your eyes and picture yourself performing the routine perfectly in your head. When it comes time to actually do the routine, the fact that you have rehearsed it in your mind's eye will give you the confidence to perform the routine without making any mistakes.

GOALS

Set goals for yourself. These can be personal goals, goals that you have as a cheerleading team, or a combination of both. Think about what it is you want to achieve as a cheerleader. Keep in mind that no goal is too big or too small: your goals could include mastering a difficult jump, learning a new dance routine, or making a particular cheerleading team.

Whatever your goals are, write them down. The act of writing down your goals will make them more concrete in your mind and may also serve as a constant reminder of what it is you are trying to achieve. Put your list of goals in a prominent place where you will look at them at least once or twice daily, such as your bathroom mirror or your locker at school.

MENTAL PREPARATION TO AVOID INJURY

INSPIRATION

It can be hard at times to stick to your goals, especially when it seems that you are a long way from achieving them or you are not progressing toward them. Combat these feelings by looking for some means to provide inspiration for yourself. When you feel inspired, this often leads to an attitude in which you believe that you can do anything you set your mind to—and indeed, you can! Inspire yourself by finding quotations or sayings that you find meaningful and writing them on small slips of paper. Post these on your bathroom mirror, around your room, or in your locker—anywhere that you need a reminder that you can achieve your goals. In fact, placing these reminders near your goals will give you a daily double-dose of

Determination and dedication help in mastering complex moves such as these, done by cheerleaders from the University of Kentucky.

CHEERLEADING

mental preparation. By reminding yourself of what your goals are and visualizing yourself achieving those goals, you will go a long way toward mastering them.

AFFIRMATIONS

In addition to writing down your goals and providing yourself with inspiration, affirmations are a good way to get yourself mentally prepared for cheerleading. These are positively-worded statements that reflect a desire or goal you have. For example, let's say this is your first year trying out for the cheerleading squad and you are understandably nervous. There are cheers to memorize, routines to learn,

Lots of practice and a positive mental attitude can go a long way toward helping you to achieve your goals as a cheerleader.

INSPIRATION

- "If you can dream it, you can do it." Walt Disney

- "Your talent is God's gift to you. What you do with it is your gift back to God." Leo Buscaglia

- "Shoot for the moon. Even if you miss, you'll land among the stars." Les Brown

- "Obstacles don't have to stop you. If you run into a wall, don't turn around and give up. Figure out how to climb it, go through it, or work around it." Michael Jordan

- "A happy person is not a person in a certain set of circumstances, but rather a person with a certain set of attitudes." Hugh Downs

- "You've got to say, 'I think that if I keep working at this and want it badly enough I can have it.' It's called perseverance." Lee J. Iacocca

and you have to come up with your own routine and perform it in front of many people—possibly even the whole school!

Rather than panicking, however, and feeling like there is no way you can possibly do it, try this: close your eyes and visualize yourself performing the cheer or routine correctly. Let your imagination run free. Imagine that everyone is clapping and cheering for you because you did such a great job. Picture yourself in the cheerleading uniform at the big football game, leading the crowds in cheers of victory. Say to yourself affirmations such as "I am a member of the cheerleading squad," and "I am performing my routines perfectly."

Notice that these affirmations are worded in the present. In other words, they are worded as if you are doing them right now, as opposed to some time in the future. This is an important key. By phrasing your affirmations in such a way, the goals are made more concrete and real in your mind. There's an old adage that says, "Fake it 'til you make it." By pretending you are a successful cheerleader and imagining yourself as such, it may not be long before your dream becomes a reality.

DON'T FORGET TO EXERCISE YOUR FUNNY BONE

All the affirmations, visualization, inspirational sayings, and other positive thinking you can conjure up may not help when you suffer a setback or a disappointment. There is no need to make light of a disappointment, such as not making the team or falling down in front of the student body when performing a cheer, but, when such things happen, it is important to keep them in perspective and maintain a sense of humor. Things could always be worse.

One cheerleader shared this story on the website cheerleading.about.com:

> It was a week before nationals, and we were practicing at the well-known GymTyme. There was a section of the cheer where we had to put up liberty, power press, heelstretch. We were making our transitions to our stunts when my right foot got caught in one of my left foot's shoe laces. I tripped horribly, falling to my face! (It was a padded floor so it was no big deal.) One of my fellow cheerleaders tried to save me from that embarrassing fall, but all she did was pull

MENTAL PREPARATION TO AVOID INJURY

my pants down … and my boxers! We were also sharing the floor with three-time national N.C.A. champions. I pulled my clothing back up fast, but it wasn't quick enough to spare me the embarrassment of showing myself … everyone in the gym that saw was laughing.

Now, while this was certainly embarrassing, the point is that it was not the end of the world. It helps to have a sense of humor in cheerleading, as well as in life. Often, being able to laugh at yourself helps you stay focused and motivated.

These high school cheerleaders demonstrate one of the first things that all cheerleaders learn: always smile and keep a positive attitude, no matter what goes wrong.

Warm-Up Exercises to Avoid Injury

Cheerleaders are often required to perform amazing jumps, splits, and other gymnastics routines. If they were not warmed up properly, these could lead to serious injury. This chapter describes a sampling of exercises to warm up cheerleaders from head to toe.

When performing these stretches, it is important to keep a few things in mind:
- Each stretch should be held for a minimum of ten seconds. You can increase your flexibility by holding the stretches for longer periods of time—for example, twenty to thirty seconds.
- Do not bounce or jerk your muscles when you are stretching. This can tear or sprain muscles.
- Do not rush through your stretches simply to be done with them. This does your body no good and can lead to injury. Always make sure that you take the time to warm up properly.
- Listen to your body and respect your limits. A small amount of discomfort is expected when stretching. If something causes you excessive pain, stop immediately. Do not compare your stretching ability to anyone else's; everyone has their own particular abilities.

Warming up properly before engaging in cheerleading can help to keep you from injury and ensure that you give the best performance possible.

NECK

1. This exercise stretches the neck muscles from side to side. Stand with your legs shoulder-width apart. Tuck your chin into your chest and hold for ten to twenty seconds. Tilt your right ear toward your right shoulder and hold for ten to twenty seconds. Return to center. Tilt the left ear toward the left shoulder, and again hold for ten to twenty seconds. Repeat three times on each side.

2. This exercise stretches the neck muscles by rotating them gently. Stand with your feet shoulder-width apart. Slowly rotate your head to the right, and look over your right shoulder until you feel a gentle stretch. Hold for ten to twenty seconds. Bring the head to face forward again, then rotate the neck to the left, looking over the left shoulder until you feel a gentle stretch. Hold for ten to twenty seconds.

SHOULDERS AND ARMS

Cheerleading is a strenuous activity that involves stretching and waving the arms, so it is important that you take the time to thoroughly stretch your arms and shoulders:

1. Stand with your feet shoulder-width apart. Clasp your hands behind your back with your elbows fully extended. Then raise your arms as

To stretch your anterior deltoid (shoulder) muscle, grasp your left arm with your right hand and pull the elbow toward your chest; hold for ten breaths, then repeat the exercise with the other arm.

WARM-UP EXERCISES TO AVOID INJURY

high as you can until you feel a gentle stretch. Hold for ten to twenty seconds.

2. Stand with your feet shoulder-width apart. Raise both arms above your head and bend the left elbow, then grasp it with the right hand. Pull your left upper arm gently toward the middle of your body. You should feel this stretch in your triceps muscle. Hold for ten to twenty seconds.

Raise your arms above your head again, then bend the right elbow and grasp it with your left hand. Pull your right upper arm gently toward the middle of your body until you feel a gentle stretch in your triceps. Hold for ten to twenty seconds.

3. Stand with your feet shoulder-width apart. Clasp your hands behind your back, with your elbows fully extended. Lift your arms slightly and bend over at the waist, then lift your arms up even farther, if you can, and hold this stretch for ten to twenty seconds. Repeat two more times.

4. To work both the arms and the waist, stand with your feet shoulder-width apart. Clasp your hands over your head, with your elbows straight. Bend at the waist, and lean to the left until you feel a gentle stretch. Hold for ten to twenty seconds. Return to the starting position, then bend at the waist and lean to the right, again holding for ten to twenty seconds.

LEGS AND ANKLES

It is extremely important that you take the time to properly stretch your legs. It is all too easy for cheerleaders to pull or strain a muscle—even tear it—by performing high kicks, jumps, or the splits before their legs are properly warmed up. Use the following exercises as a guide.

CHEERLEADING

To stretch your quadricep muscles, stand with your feet shoulder-width apart. Grab hold of your right ankle, and pull it behind you toward your buttocks, bending the knee. Hold this stretch for ten to twenty seconds. Repeat with the left leg.

1. This exercise works on your **hamstring** muscles. Sit on the floor with your legs stretched straight out in front of you. Your feet should be about hip-width apart. Keep your legs as straight as possible, then reach forward and grab hold of either your ankles or toes, depending on your level of flexibility. Hold for ten to twenty seconds. You should feel this stretch in the backs of the knees and your lower back. Try it with your toes pointing straight up and with your toes pointing forward.

2. This stretch works the groin muscles. Sit on the floor with your knees bent and the soles of your feet pressed together. Hold your feet with your hands, then rest your elbows on your lower legs. Lean forward and try to touch your forehead to the floor while you press down on your legs. Hold for ten to twenty seconds.

3. To stretch your calves, stand facing a wall, and place your hands at about shoulder height. Place one foot in front of the other, keeping the heel of your back foot firmly on the floor. Place your weight on your forward, bent leg, and lean forward, as if you are trying to push against the wall. Hold for ten to twenty seconds.

Repeat for the other leg.

WARM-UP EXERCISES TO AVOID INJURY

4. For the second calf stretch, you need a flight of stairs or a sturdy box. First, line up your heels with the edge of the step. Then move your feet back so that the balls of your feet are on the edge of the step and the rest of your feet are hanging off the edge. (You may need to lean against something or hold onto a railing for balance.) Slowly dip your heels down, then come back up. Repeat ten times.

5. This stretch works your ankles. Stand with your legs shoulder-width apart. Point your right toe so that it is touching the ground, and roll your ankle in a clockwise direction three times. Then roll the ankle counterclockwise three times. Repeat for the left foot.

SPECIAL EXERCISES FOR CHEERLEADERS

As cheerleaders often perform moves that involve jumps, splits, and tumbling, as well as partner stunts or pyramids, there are a few additional exercises you can do to build strength in particular areas.

The key to being able to perform jumps

For a seated hamstring stretch, sit with your legs spread wide apart. Lean over your left leg, and grab hold of the toes of your left foot or ankle. Point your toes forward and hold for ten to twenty seconds. Sit up. Turn so that you are facing the center, and then lean over your right leg, grabbing hold of the toes of your right foot or ankle. Point your toes forward and hold for ten to twenty seconds.

effectively and without injury is to have a strong abdomen, legs, and arms. You can strengthen these areas by performing the following exercises.

1. The classic push-up exercise (see below) develops the strength in your chest muscles, known as the pectorals. Start in a face-down position on the floor. Your back should be level, your toes should be on the floor, and your arms should be locked with your hands shoulder-width apart. To vary this exercise, try moving your arms farther out away from the shoulders (about 6–9 in/15–23 cm) or closer to the body (about 4 in/10 cm).

2. This exercise strengthens your abdominal muscles, or "abs." Start in a standing position, feet slightly apart. Jump up into the air, bringing your knees as high as possible to the front of your body. Slap your shins at the point when you have reached the highest point in your jump. Extend your arms into a "T" shape when you land. Repeat this five times, working up to ten repetitions.

To perform effective push-ups, keep your body tight and straight, and lower yourself to the ground. Push yourself back up. Try to do seven to start with, and work up until you are doing twenty or more.

COLD MUSCLES

Kansas City Chiefs cheerleading coach Linda Rae Chappell recounts the story of one cheerleader who did not want to take the time to warm up:

At one point, trying out for the cheerleading squad was the most important thing in my life.... During each person's tryout time, the rest of us were supposed to be stretching over to the side.... Right in the middle of someone's performance, a loud pop erupted in the room. It was the sound of my hamstring ripping as I attempted the splits without stretching first ... the damage was such that I was not able to try out ... I don't know which muscle hurt the most—my hamstring or my heart.

3. For another effective abdominal exercise, sit on the floor. Lie down on your back, with your hands either in front of you or behind your head. Your legs should be stretched out straight. Raise your legs at least 2 inches (5 cm) off the floor, with your toes pointed. At the same time, lift your upper body halfway up. You should be looking something like the letter "V." Hold for ten to twenty seconds. Lower your body and legs, but do not let anything touch the floor. Repeat five to ten times.

It is also important that you work on strengthening your ankles. According to cheerleading coach Linda Rae Chappell, who coached the Kansas City Chiefs football cheerleading team, ankle injuries are the number one cause of discomfort

CHEERLEADING

and loss of participation time among cheerleaders. She recommends the following exercise to help you to strengthen your ankles:

4. You will need a large exercise band or rubber band—#107, available at most office supply stores. Place the rubber band around both feet at the base of your toes. Keep one foot still, and pull the rubber band outward and upward with the other foot. Keep your heel firmly in place, and hold for ten to twenty seconds. Return to the starting position as slowly as possible, then repeat with the other leg.

In order to perform complex dance routines and organized cheers, it is important for a cheerleader to have strong, flexible muscles.

WARM-UP EXERCISES TO AVOID INJURY

Repeat this exercise for five to ten minutes a day, working up to twenty minutes.

Wrist-strengthening exercises are also important, because the wrist is used a lot in tumbling moves as well as in partner stunts—one person balanced on another's shoulders, for example, or cheerleaders balanced in a pyramid formation. The following two exercises work on developing your wrist muscles.

5. Use a large #107 rubber band or a dumbbell weighing 1–3 pounds (0.5–1.5 kg) dumbbell. Sit in a chair with your knees bent at a 90° angle. Hold the rubber band with your palm facing down and with your forearm on your thigh. Secure the opposite end of the rubber band by looping it under your foot. Slowly bend

your wrist upward as far as possible. Hold this position for ten seconds, then lower the wrist slowly, keeping your forearm on your thigh. Repeat ten times.

6. Seated in a chair with your knees bent, position the rubber band as in the previous exercise, with your hand holding the rubber band, your forearm on your thigh, and the opposite end of the rubber band around your foot. This time, your hand should be facing palm-up. Slowly bend the wrist as far as possible, hold for ten seconds, then lower slowly. Repeat ten times.

Equipment

Cheerleading, for obvious reasons, needs no protective equipment. The best form of protection for cheerleaders is to ensure that all the muscles are properly stretched and warmed up.

That being said, however, there are some pieces of equipment that everyone associates with cheerleaders: megaphones, pom-poms, and various types of signs, as well as the ever-present cheerleading uniform, which is worn with pride. While none of these equipment items offers safety or protection, some thought should be given to the design of the uniform itself, which may help to prevent certain injuries from occurring.

Cheerleading uniforms are often a combination of a sweater, sweatshirt, skirt, vest, top, pants, or shorts. All are in the school/team colors, with a logo or some other sort of design on them. These uniforms are available at professional cheerleading supply companies, which may either come to the school to measure each cheerleader individually or provide forms directing squad members how to take their measurements.

Many schools have two or even three different types of uniforms. Which uniform is worn depends on several factors, including whether the sport is conducted inside or outside, and what the weather is like. For example, football games, especially in high school and college, are played out-of-doors and in a

The pom-pom—the eternal symbol of cheerleading—is a piece of cheerleading equipment that is instantly recognizable. Initially made out of paper, today's pom-poms are made out of vinyl.

CHEERLEADING

These University of Kentucky cheerleaders are wearing a typical uniform of the kind worn for summer sports or indoor games, such as basketball.

season in which the weather can be windy, rainy, chilly, or cold. It therefore makes sense for cheerleaders to wear a uniform that keeps them warm.

Most cheerleading uniforms for football consist of skirts or pants and a sweater, all in heavy material, such as wool or a polyester blend. Sometimes, heavy jackets and gloves are worn if the weather is especially inclement.

Basketball games, on the other hand, are played indoors, in a gymnasium that is often quite warm, thanks to all the people packed into it, the athletes, and so on. In this case, cheerleading uniforms might consist of a skirt, pants, and a short-sleeved shirt or vest. These items are made out of fabric that is lighter in weight, such as cotton or a rayon blend.

Whatever the case, the most important part of the cheerleader's uniform is the shoes, and it is here where particular attention must be paid.

SHOES

Always purchase a shoe that provides you with the maximum amount of support and comfort—remember, ankle injuries are some of the most common injuries sustained by cheerleaders. Canvas or flat-soled shoes (that is, with no shaping at all on the sole) should not be worn because they offer no support for the ankles or the arches, and this can lead to a twisted ankle, shin splints, or worse.

If you cannot find shoes that are made specifically for cheerleading, which many cheerleading supply or uniform stores offer, the next best thing is to find a shoe meant for **cross-training**, aerobics, or running. Take the time to make sure the shoe fits properly. Such shoes can be expensive, but they are well worth the cost. There may be an outlet store in your area that sells familiar brand names at discount prices.

One more consideration with regard to shoes is the addition of inserts. These are special pads that go into the shoe, offering additional comfort and support by preventing pressure on a specific part of the foot or preventing abnormal movement of the foot. They can be purchased in grocery stores, department stores, and specialty shoe stores.

CHEERLEADING

Talk to your cheerleading coach or the person who sells you the shoes to see if this is something you should consider adding to your shoes.

Because strains, twists, and pulls are common in cheerleading, it is always a good idea to have ice, plastic bags, and elastic bandages on hand so that an injury can be treated immediately. Your coach should already have such things nearby in case of an emergency, but it is always a good idea to check whether this has been done or, if you wish, supply your own.

Part of being a good cheerleader means always being prepared for an injury. Stay focused on the cheers and routines when you perform them, and notify your coach right away if you suspect an injury.

EQUIPMENT

In addition to standard equipment, such as the megaphone pictured here, it is a good idea for each cheerleader to have her own small first-aid traveling kit.

At times, you may have a limitation that prevents you from fully participating in cheerleading events. In this case, you will probably have to wear a bandage, brace, or some other form of support to keep a muscle or joint as still as possible and thereby avoid aggravating or repeatedly injuring something. For example, a cheerleader who has problems with a knee, or who is recovering from a knee injury, may wear a special knee brace and avoid doing certain tumbling moves or jumps so that she does not injure the knee any further. Someone else may wear an ankle brace to support a twisted ankle that is still healing.

These items can be considered a form of safety equipment, and it is important that you wear them exactly as your doctor orders. Do not excuse yourself from wearing them just because it makes your uniform look bulky or does not "go with" your uniform.

The most important thing is the safety and health of your body, and it is better to put up with a bulky uniform than risk serious injury. After all, you may not only aggravate your injury further, but also cause so much damage that you are not able to participate at all—perhaps even permanently.

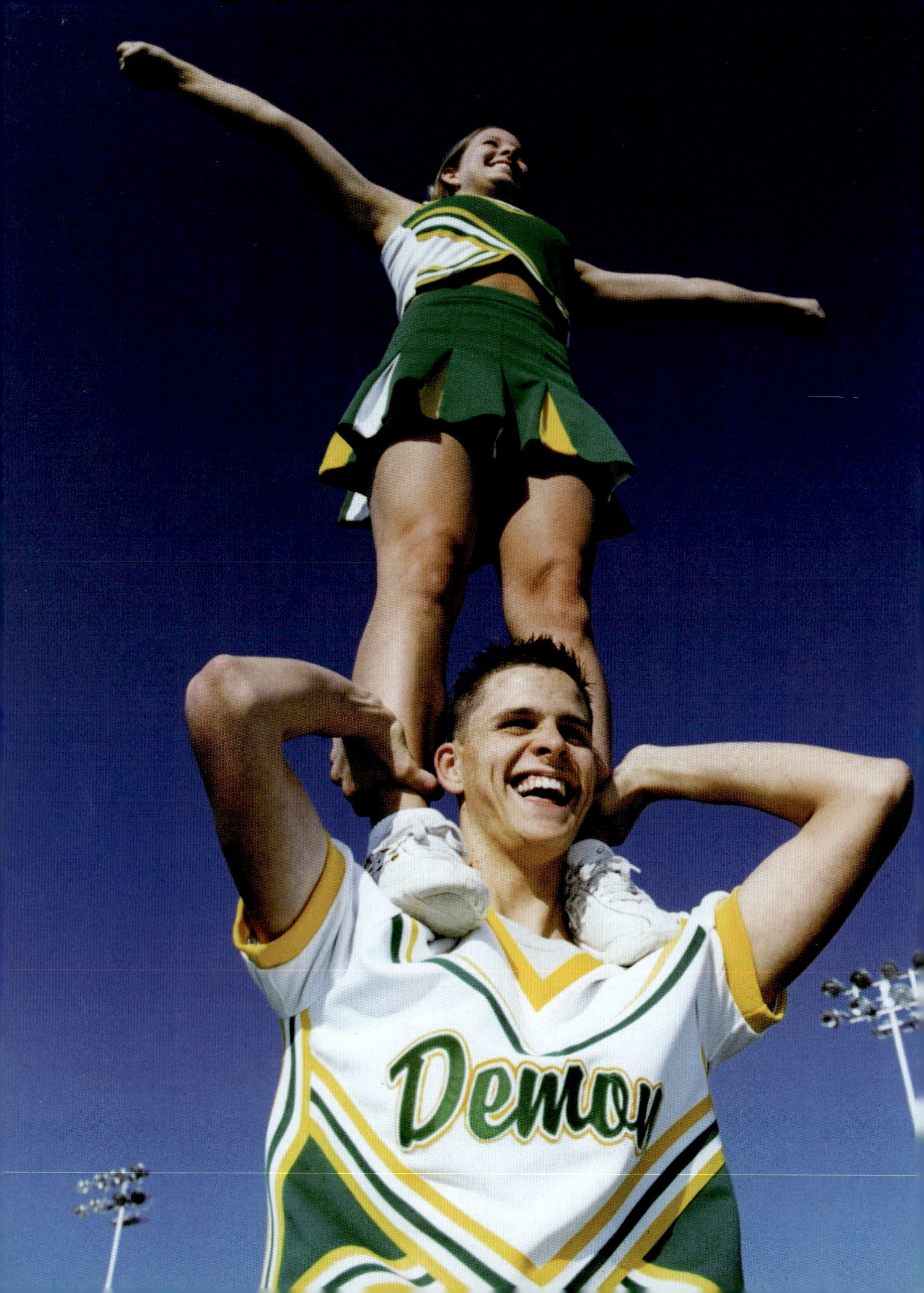

Common Injuries and Treatment

Cheerleading, like all sports, has the potential for injury. It is very important to take the time to warm up; however, even with proper preparation, injuries can and do happen.

This chapter will present an overview of some of the most common injuries suffered by cheerleaders. It is for familiarization purposes only and is not designed to take the place of a consultation with your coach or doctor.

During sporting events, there are often long periods in which cheerleaders are simply standing around, waiting, especially during football games. So, it is important to keep your muscles warm and to stay limber during these times so that you do not injure yourself when cheerleading begins again.

According to *The Sports Injury Handbook,* some of the most common injuries cheerleaders suffer are pulled muscles, inflamed tendons, and sprained **ligaments**. Hip and groin injuries also happen frequently. Furthermore, there is risk involved in such cheerleading moves as pyramids or partner stunts, such as one cheerleader standing on the shoulders of another cheerleader and then jumping, or performing some other gymnastic maneuver off their shoulders. Accidents here can cause traumatic head injuries or a broken neck. Cheerleaders have even died

Partner stunts, such as the one pictured to the left, must be undertaken only after a great deal of practice and coaching, as an injury suffered here could possibly be fatal.

CHEERLEADING

from falling from the upper part of a pyramid. As a result, some schools have moved to ban these high-risk activities.

HEAD AND NECK

When dealing with injuries to the head and neck, it is better to err on the side of caution. Such injuries are often more serious than you initially think.

Concussion is a traumatic injury to the brain, often caused by a violent blow to the head. It may upset your thinking, sight and balance, and you may even become unconscious.

People who suffer neck injuries may sometimes have to wear a cervical collar or neck brace to help the injury heal.

COMMON INJURIES AND TREATMENT

There are different categories of concussion, depending on how much force was applied to the head and at what angle the head was struck.

If the injured person regains consciousness fairly quickly, that is a good sign. Even so, the person should be monitored for symptoms such as headache, nausea, or further loss of consciousness, which can indicate bleeding inside the head.

If the loss of consciousness lasts for a long time, or if the person does not recover consciousness at all, the casualty must be taken to a hospital for treatment immediately.

Dr. Allan M. Levy, team doctor for the New York Giants, insists that under no circumstances should a person who has suffered even a minor concussion be allowed to participate in any physical activity for at least twenty-four hours after the injury.

ANATOMY OF THE NECK

The neck is a delicate area of the body, housing part of the spinal cord and vertebrae. It is extremely important that you take proper care when both warming up and performing cheerleading activities.

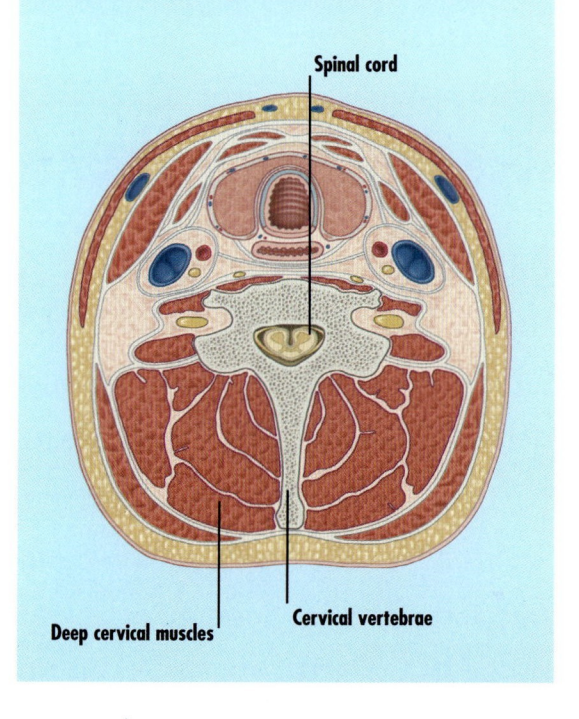

Spinal cord

Deep cervical muscles   Cervical vertebrae

It is true that an exception to this may be made in professional sports. Remember, however, concussion is an injury that causes the brain to swell up, meaning that the skull exerts pressure on it. This swelling must be given a chance

43

to completely subside because another blow—even a small one—could cause serious damage to the brain.

Sudden, violent movement may strain the muscles and ligaments of the neck, causing whiplash. This can happen if a person is pushed suddenly from behind. Whiplash can be a severe injury, and Dr. Allan M. Levy recommends that people who experience it consult a doctor, who can then perform X-rays to make sure that the delicate **vertebrae** in the neck have not slipped out of alignment or become fractured.

Whiplash is usually treated by two to three days of rest, followed by a period of physical therapy. **Anti-inflammatory** drugs are often prescribed, and some patients also need to wear a **cervical** collar, which is a high collar that supports the weight of the head, thereby taking the strain off the ligaments.

BACK

Back injuries are also common in cheerleading, and usually take the form of a muscle sprain or a ligament strain. However, back injuries can also be very serious, as when a slipped disk occurs. A person without medical training may not be able to tell how serious an injury is, so it is always best to consult a doctor when any injury occurs, and this is especially true in the case of back injuries. X-rays and other diagnostic tests may be needed to determine the exact nature of the injury.

For strains and sprains, the typical course of treatment is to keep the patient as still as possible and alternate treating the affected area with a heating pad and ice packs for fifteen to thirty minutes at a time. An anti-inflammatory medication, such as aspirin or ibuprofen, may be administered. It may also be beneficial to see a licensed massage therapist.

COMMON INJURIES AND TREATMENT

SHOULDERS

The shoulder is unique in that it is a shallow ball-and-socket joint, which means that the joint is not very stable. According to Dr. Allan M. Levy, the shoulder is the only joint in the human body that is not held together by its ligaments. Rather, the few ligaments that are there serve only to keep it from moving too far in any one direction.

ROTATOR CUFF

Rotator cuff injuries are among the most common injuries that are suffered by cheerleaders.

Supraspinatus muscle: a rotator cuff muscle that stabilizes the shoulder joint

Teres minor: rotator cuff muscle that rotates the humerus

Infraspinitus: rotator cuff muscle that holds the humerus in place

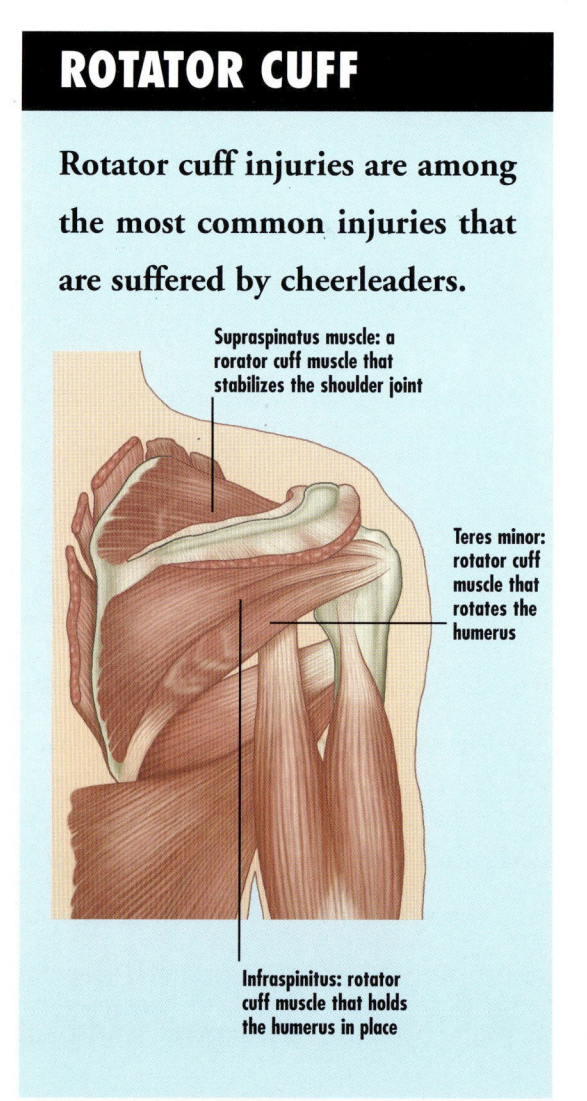

A common shoulder injury experienced by cheerleaders is what is known as a **rotator cuff** injury. Sports in which the arms are constantly brought up over the head, as in cheerleading, can cause the shoulder joint to experience too much stress, and the rotator cuff muscles can stretch out, which causes the ball of the joint to become loose within the shoulder socket. As a result, tendons rub against bone and become inflamed and painful. Most people with a rotator cuff injury report feeling pain in the biceps muscles or deep within the shoulder joint.

Rotator cuff injuries are often mistaken for a strain or tendonitis (inflamed tendons). Medication is given for the inflammation, and the

45

person is told to rest the shoulder. However, the slippage of the joint has not been treated, so pain returns when the person starts cheerleading again.

For a rotator cuff injury, it is true that the inflammation needs to be treated, but it is even more important to strengthen the rotator cuff muscles to the point that the ball of the joint is held in place and will not slip out of the socket. Often, says Dr. Levy, this course of treatment is sufficient in itself because, once the slippage stops, the inflammation goes away on its own.

WRIST

Wrist sprain is a common injury for cheerleaders. Most people actually have weak wrists because there are few muscles in this area, and it can be difficult to strengthen them.

Treating a sprained wrist typically includes keeping the joint still and rested, and applying ice packs at regular intervals for fifteen to thirty minutes at a time for three to four days. Sometimes, a soft **splint** is also required to help keep the joint still while it recovers.

GROIN

The groin muscles, known as the adductor muscles, are located along the inside of the upper thigh and serve to pull the legs together when they contract. They also help to stabilize the hip joints.

A common groin injury suffered by cheerleaders is a groin pull. A groin pull occurs when a muscle is stretched too far (which can happen when someone attempts the splits or a high kick without properly warming up first). Typical symptoms of a groin pull include pain, swelling, bruising, tenderness, and pain when stretching.

COMMON INJURIES AND TREATMENT

A groin pull is treated in much the same way as any other muscle strain: resting the injury for several days (a doctor may recommend at least one week of rest), icing the injury to reduce swelling, and compressing the injury with a compression bandage.

KNEE

The knee is a complex joint. It is an intricate network of muscle, tendons, ligaments, cartilage, and bone, which assists us in a variety of motions. According to Dr. Allan M. Levy, it is the most commonly injured joint in the body, accounting for about one-fourth of all sports-related injuries.

The most common knee injury suffered by cheerleaders and gymnasts is an

Splits such as these are not to be attempted by anyone who is not properly warmed up. Do not overextend your muscles and risk tearing them by trying to perform a cheerleading move your body is not ready for.

anterior cruciate ligament (**A.C.L.**) tear. This involves the ligaments on the front of the knee that crisscross it with the posterior cruciate ligaments, thereby providing support and stability to the knee joint. An A.C.L. tear is a serious injury, and it is not something that you can treat by yourself. This injury often occurs when severe force hits the side of the knee, when you are in the middle of a twisting motion when you fall, or when someone falls heavily against you.

If the A.C.L. is simply strained, physical therapy alone may repair the tear. If the A.C.L. ruptures and totally tears, however, surgery is usually prescribed, along with extensive physical therapy. A brace may also be worn for some time to give the knee additional support. It may be possible to return to your cheerleading activities, but only under the guidance of your doctor or coach.

KNEE LIGAMENTS

The knee is a complex joint and one of the most commonly injured joints in the body.

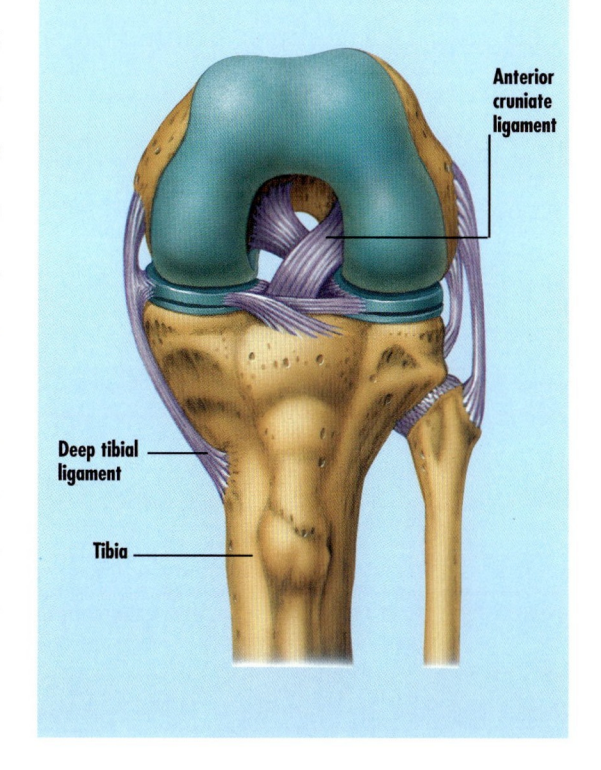

HAMSTRING

Hamstring pulls are among the most common muscle pulls, usually caused by failing to warm up properly.

COMMON INJURIES AND TREATMENT

Typical symptoms of a hamstring pull can include sharp pain and swelling, and, in the most severe tears, bruising due to internal bleeding within the muscle. You may also be unable to raise your leg straight off the ground more than a short distance without feeling pain. Typical treatment includes rest, ice, and compression: usually, resting for at least two or three days; icing the muscle for twenty minutes, three to four times a day; and wrapping the muscle in a compression bandage.

THE ANKLE

According to cheerleading coach Linda Rae Chappell, ankle injuries are the most common injury suffered by cheerleaders.

Ankles are often sprained when the ligaments are stretched too far and tear. When treating an ankle sprain, a doctor may recommend that you keep the foot rested for at least the first twenty-four hours, placing no weight on the ankle if at all possible (which may mean that you have to use crutches). An ankle sprain is often accompanied by a great deal of swelling, so you may be told to ice the ankle for twenty minutes, remove the ice for twenty minutes, ice it for twenty minutes, and so on, for at least the first forty-eight hours, or until the ankle returns to normal size. You may also be advised to wrap the ankle with a compression bandage and keep it elevated higher than your heart by propping it up on pillows at night, in order to reduce swelling and bruising. Typically, after a couple of days, you may be able to put weight on the ankle again.

As stated previously, the information in this chapter is not intended to replace the advice of your coach or doctor. For further reading, however, you may wish to consult *The Sports Injury Handbook* or the website MedTerms.com, which features a medical dictionary.

CHEERLEADING

Treating an injury as soon as possible after it happens is one of the best ways to speed up the recovery process. Here, a cheerleader has her ankle strapped to protect it against further damage.

TREATING MINOR INJURIES

CUTS

- Grab the cleanest material you can find, such as a washcloth or a strip of gauze.
- Cover the cut with the cloth, and apply firm pressure to the wound. Maintain this pressure until the bleeding has stopped.
- Next, clean the wound gently with an antiseptic and spread a thin layer of antibiotic ointment over the wound.
- If you cannot control the bleeding within minutes, seek medical help.

BRUISES

- Apply a cold compress or ice pack to the bruised area as soon as possible. Leave in place for fifteen minutes. Repeat several times a day to alleviate the pain and prevent swelling.

SPRAINS

- Immediately immerse the sprained area in ice water, or apply an ice pack for twenty minutes, to control the swelling. Repeat at twenty-minute intervals over a period of at least four hours until swelling has stopped.
- Elevate the sprained limb to at least waist level to help alleviate swelling.
- Once the swelling has stopped, soak the sprained area three times a day—first in warm water for twenty minutes, then in icy water for twenty minutes.

Source: Frandsen, Betty Rae, Kathryn J. Frandsen, and Kent P. Frandsen. Where's Mom Now That I Need Her?. *Sandy, UT: Aspen West Publishing Company, 1983.*

TEXAS
10
11:45
TIME OUTS LEFT
#4 FR-RS
PHIL
DAWSON
DALLAS
Coca-Cola
TEXAS

Careers in Cheerleading

Basically, there are two options when it comes to careers in cheerleading: you can be a cheerleader for a professional sports team, or you can become a professional cheerleading coach.

Cheerleading is a highly competitive sport, and it takes a great deal of drive and determination to become a professional cheerleader. Most of those who become professional cheerleaders have been working at it since a very young age—the average being three years old. And while there are many male cheerleaders on college and university teams, there are no male professional cheerleaders.

PROFESSIONAL CHEERLEADER

The track to becoming a professional cheerleader often begins in high school. Many professional cheerleaders report having been on their high school and college squads and having participated in dance lessons since they were very young. They have a desire to entertain and are not shy about being in front of crowds. In fact, training in dance—whether ballet, jazz, tap, or hip hop—is an integral part of becoming a professional cheerleader. Today, there are many organizations that specialize in training people to become cheerleaders, providing training in modern dance, **choreography**, and cheerleading techniques.

Many professional cheerleaders began their careers in college, such as these University of Texas cheerleaders.

CHEERLEADING

Cheerleaders often have to perform in front of huge crowds and, as this picture shows, at events such as local parades and marches.

Becoming a professional cheerleader is much like becoming a professional in any sport. To be successful, you must be determined, and you need to build up experience. Try out for your school's cheerleading team if you have not already done so. If you fail to make it the first year, try not to be discouraged. Think of this as an opportunity to further develop your skills. Take dance lessons and find people who either have been or are cheerleaders and ask them to be a **mentor** for you. By the time the next tryouts roll around, you will be ready to give it your all.

After pursuing cheerleading in high school, move on to trying out for the squad at your college or university. This is usually the next step on the path to becoming a professional cheerleader. Professional sports teams and organizations all over the

CAREERS IN CHEERLEADING

world have cheerleading squads, for football, basketball, soccer, even wrestling.

There are also organizations that offer cheerleading scholarships, such as the World Cheerleading Association (WCA), Christian Cheerleaders of America, and the U.S.A. Cheerleading Federation. Talk to your school's guidance counselor, visit the career center at your library, or talk to cheerleading coaches at the colleges you are considering in order to find out what cheerleading scholarships are available. Some of the most well-respected schools for cheerleading include

The members of a cheerleading squad often become lifelong friends, keeping in touch with each other long after their cheerleading careers have ended.

CHEERLEADING

the University of Arizona, the College of Charleston (in South Carolina), Duke University, and the University of Kentucky.

Tryouts are the most typical way to get on a professional cheerleading squad, just as is the case in high school or college. Again, you may have to go through a lot of tryouts before you finally secure a spot on a professional team, but with hard work, perseverance, and a positive attitude, you may eventually achieve your goal.

Behind every good cheerleading team is a good cheerleading coach. Often, cheerleading coaches are former cheerleaders themselves.

TRYOUT DO'S AND DON'TS

- Do study the current members of your school's cheerleading squad. The more you look and act like a member of the team, the more likely are your chances of being selected as one.
- Do be yourself. This may seem like a contradiction of the previous point. But while it is a good idea to show that you are willing to be a team player, it is also important that you stay yourself.
- Do practice cheerleading moves and dance routines at home. Practicing in front of a mirror will help you to perfect your moves. Practicing in front of family members will help you get used to performing in front of crowds.
- Don't be a poor loser. If you don't make the team this time, do not bad-mouth the coach, the judging committee, or those who did make the team. Sometimes, people quit or get kicked off the team, and if word gets out that you are a poor loser, you are unlikely to be asked to try out for the now-vacant spot.
- Don't give up.

If you didn't make the team this year, ask the cheerleading coach what you can do to improve. Take dance and gymnastic classes. Try out as many times as you possibly can.

If you make a mistake during tryouts, just take a deep breath and start again. Your persistence and determination will be noticed and may even earn you a spot on the team.

CHEERLEADING

PROFESSIONAL CHEERLEADING COACH

The average age of most professional cheerleaders is twenty-three. Cheerleading is a sport that demands a lot from the body, which means that your career as a professional cheerleader will usually be over by the time you are in your mid-thirties. This does not mean that your career in the sport of cheerleading has to end. Many people who have had successful careers as cheerleaders go on to become successful cheerleading coaches. Nor do cheerleading coaches focus just on professional sports. Coaches are needed for a wide range of ages, from middle school all the way up through college.

Again, professional cheerleading coaches arrive at this job largely by way of passion, devotion, and a determination to serve the sport of cheerleading. If you decide in high school or college that you want to be a cheerleading coach, consider taking courses in **anatomy**, **physiology**, physical education, dance, and physical therapy. In addition, consider getting a teaching certificate with a concentration in physical education, as many cheerleading coaches in schools and universities are also teachers.

Being a professional cheerleading coach is a serious endeavor, and the sport demands a lot from squad members and coaches alike. According to cheerleading coach Linda Rae Chappell, there are several key components to being successful:

- All coaches should have a cheerleading philosophy upon which all decisions as a coach are made.
- All coaches should have a firm passion for cheerleading.
- The goal of every cheerleading coach should be to help cheerleaders develop physically, psychologically, socially, and academically.
- Coaches should try to be the best role model possible for their cheerleaders.

The state of Texas just may be the cheerleading capital of the world. Many a high school or university cheerleader in this state goes on to cheer for professional teams.

Glossary

A.C.L.: The anterior cruciate ligament, which is situated at the front of the knee below the knee cap.

Affirmation: A positive assertion.

Anatomy: The study of the structures of organisms.

Anti-inflammatory: Any medication that reduces swelling.

Cervical: Relating to the neck.

Choreography: The composition and arrangement of dances.

Cross-training: Fitness training in different sports.

Fraternity: A student organization, often secret, which functions as a social club.

Hamstrings: The group of three muscles at the back of the thigh, which are connected to the knee by the hamstring tendons. Butchers once hung slaughtered pigs by these tendons—hence the name.

Ligament: A short band of tough body tissue, which connects bones or holds together joints.

Megaphone: A cone-shape instrument used to intensify or direct the voice.

Mentor: A trusted counselor or guide who advises.

Physiology: A branch of biology dealing with the processes of life and living organisms.

GLOSSARY

Rotator cuff: The group of muscles holding the shoulder joint in place, enabling the rotational movement of the arm.

Splint: A device used to protect and immobilize a body part.

Vertebrae: One of the bony or cartilaginous segments making up the spinal column.

Further Information

USEFUL WEB SITES

All About Cheerleading contains a wide range of information about cheerleading—nutrition and fitness, common injuries and how to avoid them, cheerleading scholarships, and much more: www.cheerleading.about.com

Cheer Athletics contains information on training for squads, tryouts, and invitational meets: www.cheerathletics.com/ca/history.htm

Cheerleading in Britain: www.cheerleading.org.uk/handbook/history.htm

World Cheerleading Association: cheerwca.com

The Web sites listed on this page were active at the time of publication. The publisher is not responsible for Web sites that have changed their address or discontinued operation since the date of publication. The publisher will review and update the Web sites upon each reprint.

FURTHER READING

Chappell, Linda Rae. *Coaching Cheerleading Successfully.* Champaign, Illinois: Human Kinetics, 1997.

Golden, Suzi J. *101 Best Cheers: How to be the Best Cheerleader Ever!* Memphis, Tennessee: Troll, 2001.

McElroy, James T. *We've Got Spirit: The Life and Times of America's Greatest Cheerleading Team.* New York: Simon & Schuster, 2001.

Scott, Kieran. *Ultimate Cheerleading.* London: Apple, 1998.

Wilson, Leslie. *The Ultimate Guide to Cheerleading: For Cheerleaders and Coaches.* Roseville, California: Prima Publishing, 2003.

FURTHER INFORMATION

THE AUTHOR

Lisa McCoy, a former cheerleader, is a freelance writer and editor living in Washington State. Her work covers a wide range of industries, and she has published more than a dozen titles. For a recent short story, she garnered an Honorable Mention in the L. Ron Hubbard's Writers of the Future contest, and she is now at work on a fantasy novel.

THE CONSULTANTS

Susan Saliba, Ph.D., is a senior associate athletic trainer and a clinical instructor at the University of Virginia in Charlottesville, Virginia. A certified athletic trainer and licensed physical therapist, Dr. Saliba provides sports medicine care, including prevention, treatment, and rehabilitation for the varsity athletes at the University. Dr. Saliba holds dual appointments as an Assistant Professor in the Curry School of Education and the Department of Orthopaedic Surgery. She is a member of the National Athletic Trainers' Association's Educational Executive Committee and its Clinical Education Committee.

Eric Small, M.D., a Harvard-trained sports medicine physician, is a nationally recognized expert in the field of sports injuries, nutritional supplements, and weight management programs. He is author of *Kids & Sports* (2002) and is Assistant Clinical Professor of Pediatrics, Orthopedics, and Rehabilitation Medicine at Mount Sinai School of Medicine in New York. He is also Director of the Sports Medicine Center for Young Athletes at Blythedale Children's Hospital in Valhalla, New York. Dr. Small has served on the American Academy of Pediatrics Committee on Sports Medicine for the past six years, where he develops national policy regarding children's medical issues and sports.

Index

Page numbers in *italics* refer to photographs and illustrations.

accidents *see* falls; injuries
affirmations 20–2
ankle injuries 31–2, 37, 49, *50*

back injuries 44
Baltimore Colts 11
basketball 12, 37
Berry, Halle *13*
Bush, George W. 13, *14*

Campbell, Johnny *8*, 9
camps 11
career development *52*, 53–7, *58*, 59
cervical collar *42*, 44
Chappell, Linda Rae 31, 49, 59
Cheerleaders All America awards 11
cheerleading
    history *8*, 9–15
    international appeal 14
    sports covered 12, 14
    statistics 15
Christian Cheerleaders of America 55
coaches 15, 38, 48, 49, *56*, 57, 59
colleges
    importance of cheerleading 11, *58*
    scholarships 55–6
Collegiate Cheerleading Championships 14
competitions 11, 14–15
concussion 42–4

Dallas Cowboys 12, 14
dancing 14, 17, 53, 54, 57
doctors 43, 44, 46, 47

equipment 10, *34*, 35–9
exercises, warm-up *24*, 25–33, 41, *47*

falls 41–2 *see also* injuries
famous cheerleaders 13, 14
football 12, 35–7
footwear 37–8

Gastoff, Fred 10
goals 18

groin injuries 46–7
gymnastics 11, 17, 57

head injuries 41, 42–4
Hurkimer, Laurence "Hurkie" 11

injuries
    ankle 31–2, 37, 49, *50*
    common 41–2, 47–8
    first aid 38, *39*, 51
    head and neck 41, 42–4
    legs 27, 47–8
    muscles 27, 41, 44–6, 48–9
    shoulder 45–6
    sprains 41, 46, 49, *50*, 51
    treatment 38, *39*, 43–4, 45–9, *50*, 51
inspiration 19–20, 21
international cheerleading 14
International Cheerleading Foundation (ICF) 10, 11

knee injuries 47–8

leg injuries 27, 47–8
Levy, Dr. Allan M. 43, 44, 46, 47

megaphones 10, *11*, 35, *39*
mental preparation *16*, 17–23
muscles
    developing 29–33
    hamstring 28, *29*, 31, 48–9
    injuries 27, 41, 44–6, 48–9
    stretching 25–9

National Cheerleading Association 11
neck injuries 42, *43*, 44

organizations 10, 11, 53, 55, 62

partner stunts *41*, 41
Peebler, Thomas 9
physical therapy 48
pom-poms 10, *34*, 35
positive thinking 19–22, *23*, 57
preparation mental *16*, 17–23
Princeton University 9
professional cheerleaders
    career development *52*, 53–6, *58*, 59
    earliest 11–12
pyramids 41–2

regulations 11, *12*
routines 11, 14

safety equipment 35, 39
scholarships 55–6
Schramm, Tex 12
sense of humour 22–3
shoulder injuries 45–6
splits 25, 31, *47*
Sports Injury Handbook, The 41, 49
sprains 41, 46, 49, *50*, 51
squads 12, 14, 54–5
stretching 25–9
surgery 48

televised cheerleading 14
Texas 12, 14, *52*, *58*
training
    camps 11
    courses 15
    strength 29–33
    stretching 25–9
tryouts 54, 56, 57
tumbling 11, 17

uniforms *12*, 35–7
universities 55–6
U.S.A. Cheerleading Federation 55

visualization *16*, 17–18, 21–2

warm-up exercises *24*, 25–33, 41, *47*
women, first participation 10, 11
World Cheerleading Association (WCA) 10, 55

yells 9, 12